The
Railway
Rabbits

Berry Goes to Winterland

The
Railway
Rabbits

Berry Goes to Winterland

Georgie Adams

Illustrated by Anna Currey

Orion
Children's Books

First published in Great Britain in 2010
by Orion Children's Books
a division of the Orion Publishing Group Ltd
Orion House
5 Upper St Martin's Lane
London WC2H 9EA
An Hachette UK Company

www.orionbooks.co.uk

For Kay and Nigel Bowman,
Launceston Steam Railway

The Ripple River Valley

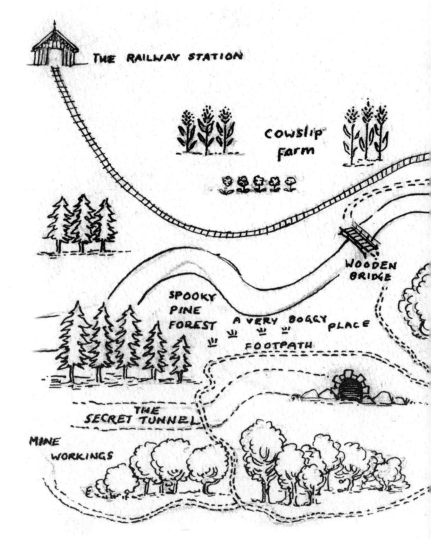

THE RAILWAY STATION

COWSLIP Farm

WOODEN BRIDGE

SPOOKY PINE FOREST

A VERY BOGGY PLACE

FOOTPATH

THE SECRET TUNNEL

MINE WORKINGS

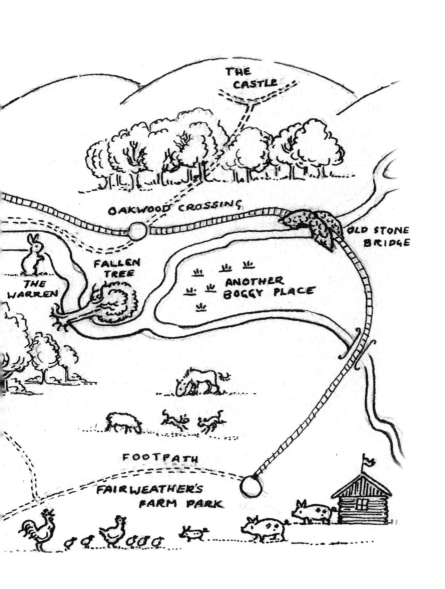

THE CASTLE

OAKWOOD CROSSING

OLD STONE BRIDGE

FALLEN TREE

THE WARREN

ANOTHER BOGGY PLACE

FOOTPATH

FAIRWEATHER'S FARM PARK

The New Tunnel

1

One cold, wintry morning, Wisher Longears woke early. She stretched her silvery-white legs and yawned. It was dark and warm in her burrow, which smelled sweetly of earth, damp leaves and rabbits. Snug in her cosy nest, Wisher felt safe tucked between winding tree roots. This was her home. She knew every twist and turn of it. Yet something was telling her the world up-burrow had changed.

Wisher crept past her brothers, Bramble, Bracken and Berry, and her sister, Fern. They were all fast asleep. Her parents were sleeping too. No need to wake them, she thought. Marr and Parr will only worry if they see me hopping off on my own!

She crawled along the burrow to the entrance, but was surprised to find it was blocked. Where there should have been daylight, Wisher saw a wall of white.

"What's this?" she said, gently patting it with her paw. It felt soft and very cold. She pushed her head through the icy crystals –

and gasped. Everything was covered in a blanket of the brightest white.

"Oh!" said Wisher. "I must be dreaming." She blinked once, then twice, just to be sure it was real. She couldn't wait to tell the others. Wisher raced back down the tunnel, calling:

"Wake up! Wake up! Come and see what's happened. Oh, you must see this. Wake up!"

Her parr, Barley Longears, sprang to his feet.

"What's the matter?" he said. "Has the roof fallen in? Are you hurt? Oh, buttercups! What a way to start the day!"

Before Wisher had time to explain, her marr woke up, her big, soft eyes open wide.

"Who's hurt?" said Mellow. "What's happened?"

Bramble, Bracken, Berry and Fern came tumbling over one another to see what all the fuss was about. At last, Wisher said:

"The roof hasn't fallen in. Nobody has been hurt. Please, come up-burrow and see!"

Barley Longears knew this part of the Ripple River Valley like the back of his paws. He knew every leaf and twig along the riverbank. This morning, it looked so different – the oak, the wooden bridge,

the meadow, the hills . . . everywhere
and everything was wearing a frosty
coat of white.

Barley could just make out the Red
Dragon's tracks running along the valley.
Snowflakes had almost covered them,
and Barley wondered if the Red Dragon
would be coming out today. Many weeks
had passed since he'd last seen the
monster, roaring up and down the valley,
belching smoke.

His thoughts were interrupted by shouts from the burrow. Barley had stopped half-in, half-out of the entrance, surprised by what he'd seen. He'd been blocking everyone's way!

"Silly me," he said, shaking his head and going outside. "Come and see the snow."

One by one, the five young Longears took their first hops into the cold. Barley watched them and worried. Their glossy coats stood out clearly against the whiteness: jet-black Bramble, gingery Bracken, red-coated Berry and soft, grey Fern. Barley looked at his own black and white fur. It was the same for him. Only Wisher, he thought, with her silvery-white coat was difficult to spot in the snow, though she'd still have to be careful.

"Watch out for foxes and Burdock

the buzzard," Barley warned them. "Our enemies will be hungry. Keen to snatch a meal. Take care!"

Mellow had been watching nearby. Barley saw her grey-brown fur, dark against the snow, and worried about her too. The safety of everyone in his family was the most important thing to him.

"Time to eat," said Mellow. "Follow me. And remember what Parr has just said. We must take extra care this morning."

Mellow led Bramble, Bracken, Berry, Fern and Wisher into the meadow. They saw how she scraped away the snow to find the grass hidden beneath. Soon, all five were pawing at the icy cold layers, eager to uncover some food.

It was hard work and Berry looked around for something easier to eat. He spotted a fir tree, its lower branches weighed down with snow.

"Look," he said, reaching up and gnawing at the bark of a branch. "Mmm! This tastes good."

But when Berry suddenly let go, it sprang up – and a big lump of snow fell on his head. *Shhlop!* The others fell about laughing at Berry in his snowy hat.

Later that morning, Barley was sitting on his favourite tree stump, keeping watch. Mellow was busy clearing a pathway through the snow to the warren. The young rabbits ran off to play.

"Don't go far," Mellow said. "And don't get up to mischief! Remember, only silly rabbits have careless habits!"

For a while, Bramble, Bracken, Berry, Fern and Wisher had fun sliding down a slope, and making a snow rabbit. They found two round stones for his eyes and a twig for his nose. When they had finished, it was nearly time to eat again.

"Let's go," said Fern. "I'm hungry."

"My paws are so cold I can't feel them," said Wisher.

Bramble, Bracken and Berry agreed. They were cold and hungry too. On their way home, they hopped, skipped and jumped about to keep warm. There was a fallen tree ahead and Berry had an idea.

"Watch me," he said. "I'm going to jump over that log."

"I wouldn't," warned Fern. "There may be something dangerous on the other side."

"Like what?" said Berry.

"Like a fox," said Bracken.

"Anything," said Wisher.

"Show off," said Bramble. "Don't do it."

Berry wasn't going to be bossed about by Bramble. Taking a running jump, he sprang into the air. He sailed over the tree trunk and dived headfirst into a snowdrift!

"Help!" Berry shouted. "I'm stuck."

Bramble, Bracken, Fern and Wisher ran round to the other side, to see what had happened. There was a hole in the snow, where Berry had fallen through. It was quite deep.

"Silly rabbit," said Bramble. "Quick," he told the others. "Let's find something to pull him out."

They all hunted around. Bracken found some ivy, clinging to the tree trunk. It was tough, but he managed to pull off a strip of the woody creeper.

"What about this?" he asked.

"Just the thing." said Bramble. "Well done."

Bracken beamed.

The little
rescue party
took hold of the ivy,
then Bramble dropped one
end down to Berry.

"Hold tight," shouted Bramble.
"Now – PULL!"

The four of them tugged with all their strength and, after much heaving, they got Berry out of the snowdrift. Then, all at once, they fell over backwards!

From his tree stump Barley was keeping a careful eye on Burdock. He had seen the buzzard circling up ahead – wings outstretched, floating on the air – just waiting for his chance to attack some small creature. Barley turned away from Burdock for a moment to see where the young rabbits were, twitching his ears for any sound of their voices. They weren't by the big oak, or over by the bridge. Where have they got to? he wondered. He was beginning to feel a little worried, when he heard someone say:

"Good morning, Barley Longears. Snow, eh? First fall this winter."

It was his friend, Blinker Badger.

"Hello, Blinker," said Barley. "Yes, lots of snow. I think there's more to come too."

"I have some news," said Blinker.

"Good or bad?" said Barley, keeping one eye on Burdock, who was flying further along the valley.

He was still listening out for the children too.

"Exciting news!" said Blinker. "As you know, I live in Oak Wood. I often walk from the wood to the river. I use the same path my family have used for years and years. The problem is, Barley, the path crosses the Red Dragon's tracks at Oakwood Crossing."

"Hm! A dangerous business," said Barley.

"Indeed it is," said Blinker. "I risk my life every time I cross his tracks. I can't change my ways. It's a badger thing, you see. But this morning – guess what?"

"What?" said Barley, wondering if Blinker would ever get to the point of his story.

"This morning I went *under* the tracks. Through a TUNNEL! It was just the right size. Ha! Can't imagine why I didn't think of making a tunnel myself."

Barley scratched his head.

"Who *did* make the tunnel?" he said.

"I'm not sure," said Blinker. "I saw some people-folk digging there the other day. It's possible they built it."

"Hm? People-folk digging tunnels," said Barley.

"Whatever next? They'll be taking over our burrows if we're not careful."

Blinker chuckled.

"You'll worry your ears off one day, Barley Longears!"

Then Blinker returned home, leaving a trail of paw prints behind him.

Snow
Tracks
2

Berry shook snow from his ears. After
falling headfirst into the snowdrift he was
cold, but cheerful. He grinned.

"That was fun!"

"Not if we hadn't pulled you out,"
said Bramble. "Lucky I was here to take
charge."

"Yes, Bramble," said Bracken.
"You were brilliant."

"You could have been stuck down
there for EVER," said Fern.

"Thanks, everyone," said Berry. "You were great."

Nobody seemed to notice that Wisher wasn't with them any more, even though she had been there to help. They were used to her hopping off on her own.

"Race you home," said Bramble to the others. "Ready, steady . . . GO!"

Bramble and Bracken got off to a flying start, leaving Berry and Fern trailing behind. They hadn't gone far, when something caught Fern's eye. She stopped, and Berry waited.

"Paw prints," said Fern, pointing to some large tracks in the snow.

"Let's follow them," said Berry excitedly.

"No," said Fern. "What if it's a dangerous animal? Parr warned us there were foxes about. These might even belong to Burdock!" Fern looked nervously about, then she said: "What do you think, Wisher?"

There was no reply.

"She's probably gone home," said Berry.

Fern wasn't so sure.

"What if she hasn't?" she said. "What if she's been caught by . . ."

Berry took a closer look at the paw prints. He was a bit worried now. The tracks were quite big. He imagined what the animal might look like. Snarling jaws? Sharp teeth? Long claws?

He saw the frightened look on Fern's face, and tried not to show what he was thinking.

"You know Wisher," he said. "She's probably wandered off, daydreaming, as usual. But maybe we *should* follow these tracks. Just in case she needs our help . . ."

 Wisher was tumbling backwards down a hill, rolling over and over and over. She curled herself into a ball, shutting her eyes tight as she gathered speed. By the time she reached the bottom, Wisher looked more like a snowball than a rabbit!

Just when she thought she'd never stop
rolling, Wisher's snowball suddenly went
bump! – and fell apart.

She stood up and brushed snow from
her fur. Then she looked around for the
others. Wisher had no idea how far she'd
rolled. Everywhere here looked sparkling
white too.

"Bramble! Bracken! Berry! Fern!"
she called. "Where are you?" Nobody
answered. Instead she heard a muffled
cry. It was coming from beneath her
crushed snowball.

"Hey! What's going on up there?"

The snow heap shook, and out popped a whiskery snout. Paws with long, sharp claws pushed the snow aside, then an animal with velvety-black fur pulled himself free. He blinked his tiny eyes at Wisher, and smiled.

"Oh, it's you," he said.

"Parsley!" cried Wisher. "I'm so glad to see you."

She'd first met Parsley Mole in the spring, and they had been friends ever since.

"All alone?" said Parsley.

"I think so," said Wisher. "Everything looks different in the snow. I'm not sure how to get home."

"Again?" said Parsley. "You're always getting lost, Wisher Longears! Tunnels, remember? I've said it before, and I'll say it again. Tunnels are the best way to get about. Rain. Snow. Summer. Winter. Come with me. I'll show you the way."

Wisher followed Parsley down a hole into his tunnel. Parsley's passageways were narrower than her own burrows, but Wisher was a small rabbit and she managed quite well. It wasn't long before they came out at the big oak, a few hops from the Longears' warren.

"Thank you, Parsley," said Wisher.

"See you again soon," said Parsley.
"Up the Burrowers!"

Then he was gone.

Mellow had been waiting near the
entrance to her burrow, when Sylvia
Squirrel stopped for a chat.

"Have you seen Wisher?" Mellow asked
Sylvia. "Or Berry? Or Fern? They've been
gone such a long time. I can't *think* what's
happened."

"Sorry," said Sylvia. "Can't say I have.
Youngsters, eh? They're such a worry.
Always up to something. I shouldn't be
surprised . . ."

Just then, Mellow caught sight of
Wisher hopping through the snow.

"There you are!" said Mellow crossly.
"I've been looking everywhere for you.
Where are Berry and Fern?"

"I thought everyone had gone
home without me," said Wisher.

"Bramble and Bracken came back a
while ago," said Mellow.

"Dear me," said Sylvia. "Such a worry for
you, Mellow. I'll keep a look-out for Berry
and Fern. Now, I must be on my way."

As Wisher followed her marr into their warren, her ears began to tingle. It was a feeling she'd had before – and each time it had been a warning that something was wrong. Wisher was afraid that Berry and Fern were in danger.

"How can I help them?" she said. "Oh, what can I do?"

Berry and Fern were making slow progress through the snow. They had followed the large paw prints over the little wooden bridge.

Ahead of them they saw a steep embankment.

"I remember going up there on our very first day up-burrow," said Berry.

"And I remember what we found at the top," said Fern "The Red Dragon's tracks! Let's go back, Berry. *Please.* "

"We can't give up now," said Berry. "Look, the paw prints go along by the river. We'll be okay."

But in a clearing, where there was no cover, they had a very scary moment. Burdock suddenly swooped towards them from the sky. He had spotted Berry's reddish-brown coat against the whiteness of their snowy surroundings. Burdock dived once, and missed. Then he soared into the air, ready to dive again.

Berry and Fern stayed still as stones, their little hearts pitter-pattering with fear. When they saw Burdock fly up, Berry knew what to do.

"Run for it, Fern," he said. "Now!"

They raced for cover – a hole, a hedge, anywhere to hide. And the first thing they saw was the tunnel.

The Santa Special
3

The cats, Florence and Skittles, had lived at the Ripple Valley Steam Railway Station for as long as anyone could remember. Many years ago they had come upon the station, quite by chance – two lost kittens with nowhere to go – and decided to stay. The people-folk at the Railway were very kind. They gave Florence and Skittles plenty to eat and a warm place to sleep next to the Booking Office stove. The two cats were as much a part of the station as

the train, the signals and the track, and
the passengers liked to see them around.
It was, as Florence often reminded
Skittles, a Purrfect Arrangement.

At about midday Florence plonked
herself down in the middle of the Booking
Office to wash. She took pride in keeping
her smooth black coat and neat white
paws clean, and seemed unaware of the
passengers weaving around her. They
were trying not to step on her tail!

Skittles was sitting in his favourite
place, gazing out of the window. He
was a tabby with a smudgy black nose.
He thought the station
was especially
busy today. There
seemed to be more
children than
usual too.

There wasn't much Skittles didn't know about the railway. It hadn't taken him long to work out the Timetable – the comings and goings of the big, red steam engine, Spitfire Number 47512.

"It's simple," he had explained to Florence once. "The train runs up the line and back again, twice before lunchtime. The same again before tea."

Today, however, was different. Skittles had found out that there would be only one train ride to the Farm Park – the Santa Special. It would be carrying a Very Important Passenger. He told Florence all this, while she was washing.

"Fascinating," said Florence, looking at her left front paw, then giving it one last lick. "Come on. Let's go and see them off."

40

The cats went to sit near an open carriage, listening to the excited chatter of some boys and girls. They overheard snippets of conversations:

"Father Christmas . . . Winterland . . . sleigh . . . reindeer."

Florence and Skittles had been around people-folk long enough to understand some of the things they said. But today it was all very puzzling. They had no idea what they were talking about.

Just then, the children started cheering. The two cats turned to see a very large man with a beard, dressed in red. He was carrying a large sack and laughing:

"Ho! Ho! Ho!"

The cheerful man came over to Florence and Skittles. He was holding two little collars, each with a tiny silver bell.

"One for Florence," said the man in red, stooping to put it on. "And here's one for Skittles. Merry Christmas!"

The cats purred and purred with delight, then walked up and down the platform, showing off their new collars.

"Who's that man?" said Skittles.

"I have no idea," said Florence.

A few minutes later, they saw him step aboard the Santa Special to more cheers from the passengers. He got into the last carriage, and put his sack at the back.

The engine gave a loud whistle –
Whoooo-Wheeep! – and the guard waved
her flag. Then Florence and Skittles
watched the train clatter slowly down the
line, on its way to Oakwood Crossing and
beyond.

"It's snowing again," said Florence.
"Brrr! Let's go inside."

"I'm scared," said Fern. "I don't like this
tunnel. It's creepy."

"Stay close," said Berry. "Look, it's not
far to the other end."

After their escape from Burdock,
Berry had been leading the way through
the tunnel they'd spotted. The two had
lost sight of the paw prints when they'd
entered the tunnel, but Berry hoped to
find them again. As they approached the

other side, they saw tracks ahead.

"They look like the same paw prints," said Fern.

"Whoever made them is heading for the wood," said Berry. "Wisher may be . . ."

He stopped. There was a thundering, rumbling sound just above their heads. The noise inside the tunnel was deafening. The ground shook. Fern trembled. Overhead, a loud whistle was followed by a terrible screeching sound, which went on and on.

"Is-is that what I think it is?" said Fern, shaking from the tip of her ears to her tail.

Berry nodded. He was scared too.

"The Red Dragon!" he said. He remembered Wisher telling him about how she'd come close to the monster once before, and what it had felt and sounded like.

"I think he's stopped," whispered Fern.

The thundering noise had been replaced by hissing.

"I'll go and see what's happening," said Berry bravely. "Stay here."

"Don't leave me on my own," said Fern. "I'm coming."

They crept out of the tunnel into steamy clouds. Towering above them, the Red Dragon looked even bigger than they'd imagined. He was puffing sooty black smoke.

"He looks very angry," said Berry, daring to peep at the gigantic beast. He caught a glimpse of some flames and was very frightened.

"I think he's stuck," said Fern. "I can see people-folk. They're clearing snow from his tracks."

"No wonder he's so cross," said Berry.

"Quick! Let's go," said Fern. "Before he catches us."

"We can't leave, not till we've found Wisher," said Berry. "We have to follow those paw prints. Anyway, remember what Parr always told us? The Red Dragon never leaves his tracks. We'll be okay as long as we keep away from them."

Berry went ahead of Fern. He had taken only a few hops, when he saw something lying at the bottom of the embankment. He scrambled down the bank for a closer look.

"There's something here," he called to Fern.

Berry saw what looked like a large pouch, and some animals lying in the snow. There was a rabbit with silvery-white fur, just like Wisher. Her eyes were open wide. She lay very still.

"Oh, Wisher!" Berry cried. "Wake up!"

Fern went to help him.

"The animal we were tracking must have caught her!" she said.

"And when he saw the Red Dragon, he dropped her and ran away," said Berry.

They bent over to lift Wisher.

"Poor Wisher," said Fern. "I think she's frozen. That's why she can't speak."

At that same moment, two hands grabbed Berry and Wisher from behind. Fern was so surprised, she rolled over backwards – out of sight and out of reach. She saw a human dressed all in red, sling the pouch over his back, then climb on to the Red Dragon. The Dragon gave a loud whistle, and Fern watched as it carried Berry and Wisher away.

Jingle Bells
Jingle Bells!
4

It was a busy time at Fairweather's Farm
Park. Fred Fairweather had brought his
animals into the barn, just before the first
fall of snow. It was a large barn, open on
two sides, where his sheep and pigs could
shelter from the wintry weather.

Among them was Mrs Woolly, a ewe
who liked to know everything that was
going on around the farm. Within a few
minutes of settling into her comfortable,
straw-filled pen, Mrs Woolly put her

head over the side to speak to her neighbour, Agatha Old Spot.

"Goodness," said Mrs Woolly. "You look a bit squashed. You're a large pig, Agatha, and with seven piglets . . ."

"We have plenty of room, thank you," said Agatha. She looked proudly at her piglets, who were playing hide-and-seek in the straw. Foster was her special favourite. He was, she thought, a particularly fine pig. "I'm glad to be out of the cold."

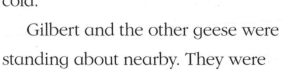

Gilbert and the other geese were standing about nearby. They were

sometimes allowed
to roam around the
farmyard. Gilbert
overheard what Agatha
had said.

"Cold?" he said. "Not a
bit-bit-bit of it. It'll be snowing soon.
Luverly-uverly-uverly!"

"Bah!" said Mrs Woolly. "Never mind
the weather. Look. Something's going on
over there. I've never seen this before.
What's happening?"

Everyone turned. They saw Fred and
Jim, the farm-hand, putting up a giant fir
tree in the middle of the yard. The tree
was so tall, it was difficult to see the top
of it.

"It's as high as the barn roof," said
Foster.

"What's it for?" said Mrs Woolly. "That's
what I'd like to know."

All the farm animals watched as the men strung lights through the branches and decorated the tree with shiny, coloured balls. When it was finished, Foster thought the pretty baubles looked like fruit. I wonder if they're good to eat? he thought. Which reminds me, I'm hungry! His tummy rumbled.

"Is it nearly lunchtime?" he asked his mother hopefully.

Agatha smiled. It was so like Foster to be thinking about his next meal.

"Yes," she said. "Not long now, you'll see."

Gilbert's weather forecast came true. There was a heavy snowfall that night and much excitement at the Farm Park next morning. Gilbert and the geese honked happily:

"Snow, snow. Told you so-so-so!"

Foster, who'd never seen snow before, wondered what it tasted like. He pushed his snout under the side of his pen to lick a lump, but he was disappointed.

"It doesn't taste much of anything," he told the other piglets. "I can't wait for breakfast."

That afternoon, Mrs Woolly was surprised by the arrival of two new animals.

"No one told *me* they were coming," she said. "There's a lot going on I don't understand. Who are these creatures?"

Peering closer at the newcomers, Mrs Woolly could see they were wearing harnesses hung with cowbells. The bells clanged whenever they moved. *Cling! Clang! Clong!* Mrs Woolly heard Agatha snoring next door.

"Wake up," she said. "You must see this. Oh, Agatha, do wake up!"

Grunting loudly, Agatha rose to her trotters. "Wha-what is it?" she said sleepily.

"There," said Mrs Woolly. "Have you ever seen such an odd-looking pair?"

"Sssh," said Agatha. "I think they're coming over."

They watched Fred lead the animals to a water trough near the barn, then leave them to have a drink. *Slurrrrp! Slurrrrp! Slurrrrp!*

Mrs Woolly coughed.

"Excuse me," she said. "Who, er, *what* are you?"

"Us?" said one. "I'm Rufus and this is my friend, Rodney."

"We're reindeer," said Rodney.

"RAIN . . . *dear*?" said Mrs Woolly. "Nonsense! It's snowing."

"I think they said 'REINDEER'," said Agatha.

"Hee, hee, hee," laughed Rufus and Rodney, which set their cowbells jangling.

Cling-clang-clong! Cling-clang-clong!

"Stop!" cried Mrs Woolly. "You'll give me a headache. What are you doing here?"

"Doing?" they said. "Can't you see? We're having a drink."

"Yes, yes," snapped Mrs Woolly. "What I mean is, why have you come to Fairweather's? And why hasn't your cart got any wheels?"

Rufus sighed.

"If you must know," he said, "we're

waiting for Father Christmas. He should have been here by now."

"And this is his *sleigh*," said Rodney. "Sleighs don't have wheels. I thought everyone knew that."

The reindeer started to laugh again. Mrs Woolly glared.

"Who is Father Christmas?" she asked.

Before Rufus or Rodney could reply, a cheery whistle sounded from not far away.

Whooo-Wheeep!

Mrs Woolly was surprised to hear it. She knew the train didn't usually run at

this time of year. However, she was keen to show the newcomers that she did know something.

"That's the train," she said. "It's bringing visitors to the Farm Park."

"And Father Christmas," said Rufus.

"With any luck," said Rodney.

There was no time for further explanation, because Fred returned to collect the reindeer.

"Time to meet the Santa Special," he said. "We must welcome everyone to Winterland!"

"Winterland?" said Mrs Woolly to Agatha. "I've never heard the farm called that before."

Agatha yawned.

"Very strange," she said.

Rufus and Rodney said goodbye, and went off jangling their bells. Agatha settled herself for another nap, but Mrs Woolly stayed wide-awake. She didn't want to miss a thing.

"I want to see what this Father Christmas looks like," she said. "Whoever he is."

From her pen, Mrs Woolly had a very good view of Fairweather's railway station and the platform.

The gleaming red engine, Spitfire, had just arrived with four small carriages full of passengers.

Mrs Woolly checked everyone as they climbed off the train. There were more children than grown-ups today, she noticed. At last, a big man with a bushy white beard, dressed all in red, stepped on to the platform. I wonder if this is Father Christmas? she thought.

Mrs Woolly was still wondering, when she was deafened by the sound of singing blasting across the yard:

"Jingle bells,
jingle bells,
jingle all the way . . ."

To make matters worse, Gilbert and
the geese strutted about honking horribly.

Honk, honk, honk!

"What a noise!" cried Mrs Woolly.

Agatha groaned.

"I was trying to sleep," she said.

The piglets were enjoying themselves.

"This is fun!" cried Foster.

They danced happily round and
round in time to the music.

"Jingle bells,
jingle bells,
jingle all the way . . ."

The Sack of Toys

5

Berry could hardly breathe. His nose was squashed and somebody, or something, was sitting on his ear. He glimpsed a white paw and thought it must be Wisher's.

"Wisher?" he whispered.

There was no reply. Berry's heart thumped loudly.

The events of the past few minutes flashed by as he remembered what had happened.

"I was following paw prints with Fern," he said to himself. "We'd just found Wisher in the snow, near the tunnel. I *think* it was Wisher. She was asleep and I tried to wake her. Then we were grabbed by the Red Dragon!"

Berry's head was spinning. He was frightened and confused. For a moment he listened to the sound of the Red Dragon rattling along his tracks – *Clickety-clack, clickety-click-clickety-clack.* A shiver of fear ran down his spine. He wondered if the monster ate rabbits.

"Wisher, can you hear me?" he whispered, more urgently this time. "Are you awake?"

Again, she didn't answer. Berry shifted sideways to look at her. The white rabbit toppled over and, for the first time, Berry could see her properly. This rabbit was bigger than Wisher and she was wearing a green ribbon.

"Oh, you're not my sister," he said. "I'm Berry Longears. What's your name?"

She didn't twitch a whisker.

"Hm? You're not very friendly," said Berry. "But if you're not Wisher, where *is* she?" He couldn't think what could have happened to her.

From his cramped position, Berry saw some other creatures. There was a pink cat and a blue spotted dog, smiling at him.

"What's so funny?" said Berry. "We've been caught by the Red Dragon. Aren't you scared?"

The cat and the dog stared back as if he wasn't there.

"Why won't you speak to me?" said Berry. "What's wrong?"

Then all of a sudden he realised.

"Creeping caterpillars!" he exclaimed. "You're not frozen, are you? It's the Red Dragon. What's he done to you? Help! I'll be next. I've got to get out of here!"

Just then, the Red Dragon went round a bend, blowing his whistle. *Whooo-Wheeep!* The monster was slowing down. *Click-er-ty-clack, click-er-tee-clack* – the sounds got slower and slower, until they stopped.

Berry spotted daylight through a hole in the pouch. This was his chance to escape.

He pushed his head through. He wriggled and squirmed. Squirmed and wriggled. But no matter how hard he tried, Berry could not ESCAPE. He was stuck with his head poking out.

Without warning Berry found himself lifted off the Red Dragon, then seconds later, dropped back down with a *bump!*

"Ooof!" said Berry, hitting his nose.

Berry saw he was now on some sort of cart. When the cart moved, it slid smoothly over the snow – *Swish-swish-swish.* He could hear the sound of bells too – *Cling-cling-cling-a-ling* – but he couldn't see where they were coming from.

The cold air felt good after being
inside the pouch. Berry was scared
and excited at the same time.
Most of all, he was glad
they'd left the Red Dragon far
behind. He tried several more
times to struggle free, then gave up.
In no time, it seemed, they were flying
past animals inside an enormous barn.
Then they were skimming round an
icy pond, and whizzing by a tree
hung with twinkling lights.
"A star tree!" Berry exclaimed.
The cart pulled up outside a large
wooden hut.

Before Berry knew what was happening, he was carried inside. There were people-folk everywhere! The man put the pouch near a table, and Berry's nose was temptingly close to a bowl of fresh green salad. By this time Berry was very hungry, he took a chance and nibbled some lettuce.

"Look!" shouted a boy. "There's a rabbit. A furry red rabbit. Please, Father Christmas. May I have the little red rabbit?"

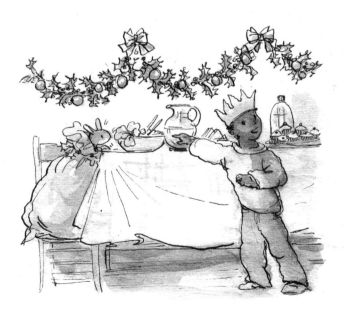

Berry froze. Father Christmas looked puzzled.

"I'm afraid I don't have a *red* rabbit," he told the boy. "But I'll see what I've got in my sack . . ."

He opened the sack and reached inside.

"There's a pink cat," he said. "And a blue dog. I'm sure I have a *white* rabbit somewhere . . ."

Unfortunately, the very next thing Father Christmas saw was Berry's fluffy white tail. He grabbed it and pulled Berry out backwards. Berry kicked and struggled with all his might.

"That's him!" shouted the boy.

"Aaaaah!" sighed the other children.

"Bless my boots!" cried Father Christmas. He was so surprised, he dropped Berry on the floor.

Berry picked himself up and ran. He darted this way, that way, slipping through children's legs trying to find a way out. It was like running through a wood of strange-looking trees. He felt a breeze. He could smell fresh air! Where was it coming from? An opening. There!

Berry raced for the gap and slipped through. Then he kept on running into the farmyard. He paused to catch his breath by the star tree. I must hide, thought Berry. Somewhere safe . . .

He saw the barn. Just the place! Once inside, he crouched near some animals. He could hear snuffles and grunts. He didn't know what the animals were, but he wasn't afraid. At least he had found cover – for the time being. What now? he wondered. He'd had a lucky escape, but he was alone and afraid. Berry began to sob. A tear trickled slowly down his cheek.

"I want Marr and Parr," he sniffed. "I want to go HOME."

Barley's Search Party
6

Fern raced back to the warren as fast as her legs could carry her – through the tunnel, over the wooden bridge and around the oak. She didn't stop, until she flopped down on the floor.

"Where were you?" said Mellow crossly. "I've looked everywhere!"

"We've been worrying our whiskers off," said Barley. "We thought Burdock . . . er, well, we didn't know what to think."

Mellow gave Fern a big hug. "Thank the stars you're safe!" she said. "Where's Berry?"

Between gasps for breath, Fern described how Berry and Wisher had been carried off by the Red Dragon. Mellow looked confused.

"What do you mean?" said Mellow gently. "Wisher is here with Bramble and Bracken."

Mellow called them and, when they came, Fern was astonished to see Wisher.

"Oh no!" she said. "Poor Berry is in trouble. And it's my fault! If only I hadn't spotted those paw prints . . ."

"Ah, yes," said Barley. "The tracks leading to Oakwood Crossing? I think you and Berry were on the trail of my old friend, Blinker!"

Fern's eyes opened wide.

"Wha–" she began.

Mellow threw up her paws.

"Enough about Blinker!" she said. "What about Berry? Where is he? What are we going to do?"

"I'll organise a search party," said Barley. "There's no time to lose. Winter days are short. It'll be dark soon. Bramble, Bracken, Wisher, come with me. Fern, you stay with Marr."

"That's not fair," said Fern. "I want to go."

"No," said Mellow firmly. "You've had quite enough adventure for one day."

Word quickly spread along the riverbank. In no time, friends were gathering at Barley's tree stump, eager to join the search party. Among the first to arrive were Sylvia Squirrel and Blinker Badger. When everyone was together, Barley told them about Berry and where he'd last been seen.

"Near the tunnel, you say?" said Blinker.

"Carried off by the Red Dragon!" said Sylvia. "Goodness knows where that monster has taken Berry. A nasty business, if you ask me."

"Yes, thank you," said Barley quickly.
"It's true. We don't know where Berry is.
Has anyone any ideas?"

Wisher had been half-daydreaming,
half-listening to this conversation and had
a faraway look in her eyes.

"Parr, my ears are tingling," she said.
"I can hear bells ringing. There are lights
whizzing around in my head. I think
Berry's near them."

Bramble rolled his eyes.

"Huh!" he said. "You and your dreams."

"I can't explain it," said Wisher. "It's just a feeling."

"Maybe Wisher knows something we don't," said Bracken. "Remember our first day up-burrow, Bramble? Wisher warned us about the Red Dragon's tracks *before* we found them."

Bramble nodded. Wisher had been right on that occasion.

Now Barley was getting impatient.

"Thank you, Wisher," he said. "It's a start. Maybe your bells and . . . er, lights will help us find Berry. Let's not waste time arguing about it. I saw Burdock hunting earlier and he's probably still about. We should get going."

"Where to?" asked Blinker.

Just then, the ground beneath them trembled, and a small mound of freshly dug earth appeared. A moment later, out from a hole popped Parsley. Wisher was very pleased to see her friend again.

"Sorry I'm late," said Parsley. "Heard about your search party, Barley. Had to come. Got held up by Daisy Duck. She was quacking on and on about some gossip from Gilbert Goose. Gilbert told her about some strange goings-on at the Farm Park. Animals wearing bells, would you believe? And a tree full of lights."

Wisher's eyes grew wide.

"There you are, what did I say?" she said. "Bells and lights!"

"Okay – you *might* be right," Bramble mumbled.

"This is excellent news," said Barley. "Does anyone know the way to the farm?"

"Daisy lives up-river," said Parsley, pointing in the direction he'd just come. "I know that's near the farm."

"Lead on, Parsley Mole!" cried Barley.

"Tunnels are the best way to get about, as I always say," said Parsley. "I'll go on ahead. You follow on top. I'll pop my head up now and again to show you the way."

"May I go with Parsley, Parr?" asked Wisher.

"Very well," said Barley. "But stay together, mind. No hopping off on your own, Wisher Longears!

If there's danger ahead, or we happen to find Berry, I'll send my usual signal." He thumped his hind foot three times on the ground. *Thump, thump, thump!*

Wisher followed Parsley into his tunnel, and followed her friend along one twisty passage after another. As promised, Parsley often burrowed to the surface, to keep the rest of the search party travelling in the right direction. For Barley, Bramble, Bracken, Blinker and Sylvia the walk through the snow was slow-going. They called Berry's name as they went, in the hope he might hear them.

After what seemed a very long time,
Bramble gave a shout:

"Look! Lights! Over there."

"You're right," said Bracken.

Barley's long ears twitched.

"I think I can hear bells," he said.
"Listen."

The sound of bells came to them,
cling-clang-clanking across the snow.
Then they saw Parsley waving to them.
Wisher was with him, pointing excitedly
to the lights ahead.

"Come on," said Barley. "Let's catch them
up. We haven't far to go now."

Fireworks
and a
Feast
7

It was Mrs Woolly who first saw Berry
running across the farmyard.

"See that?" she said to Agatha Old
Spot. "There's a rabbit heading this way.
Looks terrified, poor creature."

"Where?" said Agatha.

"Here," said Foster. He'd spotted Berry,
crouching by the pig pen. "Hello. I'm
Foster. What's your name?"

Berry wiped a tear from his eye.
Foster? he thought. I remember that name
from somewhere.

"I'm Berry," said Berry. "I'm in trouble."

"We'll help you, if we can," said Foster.

"Yes, tell us," said Mrs Woolly.

Gilbert and the geese gathered to hear Berry's story too.

"I like a good gossip," said Gilbert, settling himself comfortably in the straw. "Get on with it, young rabbity-abbity-rabbit."

Berry told everyone what had happened. When he described how he'd mistaken a strange, white rabbit for his sister, Wisher, Foster leapt to his trotters.

"I know Wisher!" he cried.

"Of course," said Berry. "I remember now. You're Foster, the runaway piglet!"

Agatha smiled. Wisher had helped Foster last springtime, and now Agatha wanted to help Berry.

"We must get you safely home," she said to Berry. "It's getting dark. Come on everybody – think."

They were thinking hard, when Rufus and Rodney arrived, clanking their cowbells.

Clang-clang-clang!

"Oh, do be quiet," said Mrs Woolly. "I'm trying to think."

"It must be difficult," said Rufus, trying not to laugh.

"For a sheep," added Rodney.

"Bah!" said Mrs Woolly, glaring at them.

A moment later, they heard a

Whoooooooosh! Weeee!
Pop, pop, pop – BANG!

"Thunder and lightning!" screeched Gilbert. "We'll all be struck down-down-down."

Berry ducked, then looked up. A shower of red, green and yellow stars was raining from the sky. The sparkling lights lit up the farmyard. He'd never seen anything like it.

Whoooooooosh! Whoooooooosh!

Suddenly Berry thought he could see moving shapes over by the farm gate.

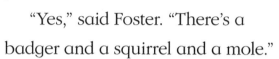

By the light from the falling stars, he saw that they were animals.

"Foster," he said. "Can you see them?"

"Yes," said Foster. "There's a badger and a squirrel and a mole."

"And rabbits!" cried Berry, above the noise. He stood up on his hind legs and counted them. "One, two, three, four. Oh, Foster! Look, there's my parr. He's with Bramble, Bracken and Wisher."

"I'm here!" cried Berry, jumping up and down and waving.

"Go on, they're waiting for you," said Foster. "Say hello to Wisher for me."

"I will," promised Berry.

"Run for it," said Agatha.

"Go-go-go," said Gilbert.

"Hop it," said Mrs Woolly. "Good luck!"

"Thank you," said Berry. "Goodbye!"

Berry ran across the yard. There were flashes and bangs all around him, but he didn't care. Nothing was going to stop him now. The next thing Berry knew, Parr was hugging him, and Bramble, Bracken and Wisher were patting him on the back. Parsley, Blinker and Sylvia were cheering and clapping their paws.

"Thank you," said Berry. "I can't believe you're all here. I didn't know how I was going to get home!"

Just then, there was another *whooosh!* in the velvety darkness, over their heads

Weeee! Pop, pop, pop – BANG!

"Time to go," said Barley, covering his ears. "Before the sky falls on our heads!"

It was a cheerful group of animals that walked back to the Longears' warren that night. Even Parsley agreed to travel above ground on this special occasion.

The moon shone brightly, and the young rabbits had fun retracing their paw prints in the snow.

"Here," said Blinker, pointing to a set of paw prints. "These are mine."

Berry took a good look.

"They're just like the ones leading to the tunnel . . ." he began. Then he stopped. He realised the prints he and Fern had followed were probably Blinker's too. Berry felt a little foolish. "We thought you were a dangerous animal."

Blinker laughed.

"Oh, but I am," he said, and chased after Berry, growling playfully. "Gr-r-r-r-r!"

Everyone laughed and they all set off again, singing as they went:

"Home we go, through the snow,
Deep as deep can be.
Berry's found, safe and sound –
A happy band are we!"

It didn't take long for news of Berry to reach Mellow. She'd sighed with relief to hear that Berry had been found, safe and well, and was on his way home. But she was horrified at some stories that were buzzing along the riverbank. It had started with Gilbert Goose.

"Have you heard about Berry Longears?" said Gilbert, when he met Daisy Duck. "Horrible-orrible-orrible.

Caught by a man with a pink beard. Chased by a blue cat. Escaped from a dog with red spots. I think I've got that right. Poor little rabbity. What a to-do-do-do!"

"Well, I never!" quacked Daisy. "I thought animals with bells was bad enough. But this is far worse. I must spread the news." She paddled off down river, and the first friend she saw was Violet Vole.

"Have you heard?" said Daisy. "Berry was caught by a blue man with spots. He had to fight a fierce red cat to escape. Then a pink dog with a beard chased him round the farm."

"I've never heard anything like it," said Violet. "I must tell Mellow Longears at once."

Mellow's eyes had grown wider and wider, as she listened to Violet. She couldn't wait to see Berry and hear what had really happened. Before then, there was much to do to welcome him home.

"Hurry, Fern," she said. "Help me carry this food up-burrow. Blinker and Sylvia are with Barley, and they're much too big to squeeze into our little warren!"

"I've never seen so much food," said Fern, her arms full of nuts and dried fruits.

Mellow smiled.

"Sensible rabbits have careful habits," she said.

She took a bunch of dandelion leaves from a hollow, tucked away at the back of the warren. "I keep a store of food for winter. There's plenty to share."

Up-burrow, Mellow and Fern cleared snow beneath a holly bush, and set out the food. Mellow thought it was a good place for a feast. The clusters of bright, red holly berries reminded her of Berry's glossy coat. She couldn't wait to see him safely home.

She looked about anxiously to see if they were coming.

"Oh, I hope they're all right," she said to Fern. "They'll be easily seen in the moonlight. A fox, or a sharp-eyed owl. At least Burdock won't be about. With any luck, he'll be sleeping. Still, if they all stay together they should be okay . . ."

"Listen," said Fern. "I can hear singing."

The sound of cheery voices, drifted towards them from across the snow-covered meadow:

". . . Berry's found, safe and sound –
A happy band are we!"

Soon afterwards, everyone was sitting under the holly bush having a wonderful time. Between mouthfuls, Berry entertained them all with his amazing story.

He'd been carried off by the Red Dragon and had lived to tell the tale. He told them about Foster and the other animals who'd tried to help him at the farm.

When he'd finished, Wisher said:

"There's one thing I don't understand, Berry. How could you mistake me for that strange rabbit in the pouch?"

Berry gave Wisher a cheeky grin.

"Well – you are a bit strange, *sometimes*," he said, then quickly, "only joking. Thanks, Wisher. Thanks, everyone. I couldn't have found my way home without you."

"Up the Burrowers, eh?" said Parsley. "Always saving the day! It's time I was going home myself. See you again soon, Wisher."

"I must be off too," said Blinker.

"And me," said Sylvia, yawning. "Goodnight."

"Time for bed, everyone," said Mellow. "It's been a long day. Quickly, into the warren all of you. Berry? Berry, where are you?"

Mellow peeped under the holly, and there was Berry. He had fallen sound asleep.